To my parents - RS
With thanks to Sue and Sarah - SH

Orchard Books, 95 Madison Avenue, New York, NY 10016

Printed and bound in Singapore

10 9 8 7 6 5 4 3 2 1

Library of Congress Cataloging-in-Publication Data

Scamell, Ragnhild.
Three bags full / story by Ragnhild Scamell ; pictures by Sally Hobson.—
1st American ed.   p.   cm.
Summary: Millie, a kindhearted sheep, gives away pieces of her wool
to other needy animals and soon finds that she has no coat left.
ISBN 0-531-05486-1
[1. Sheep—Fiction.   2. Animals—Fiction.]
I. Hobson, Sally, ill.   II. Title.
PZ7.S2792Th 1993 [E]—dc20 92-50882

Three
Bags
Full

Story by
Ragnhild Scamell
Pictures by
Sally Hobson

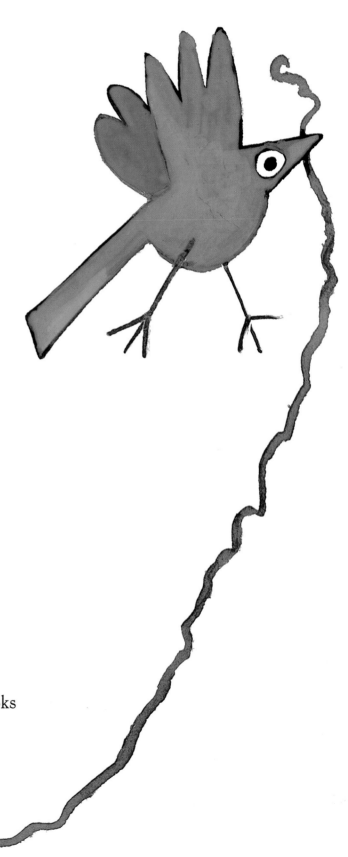

Orchard Books
New York

Millie was very, very kind.
She tried not to squash flowers
and she tried not to step on
anyone smaller than herself.

One warm spring morning, Millie was skipping around in her field, feeling happy. She sniffed a yellow flower and   almost sat on a bird.

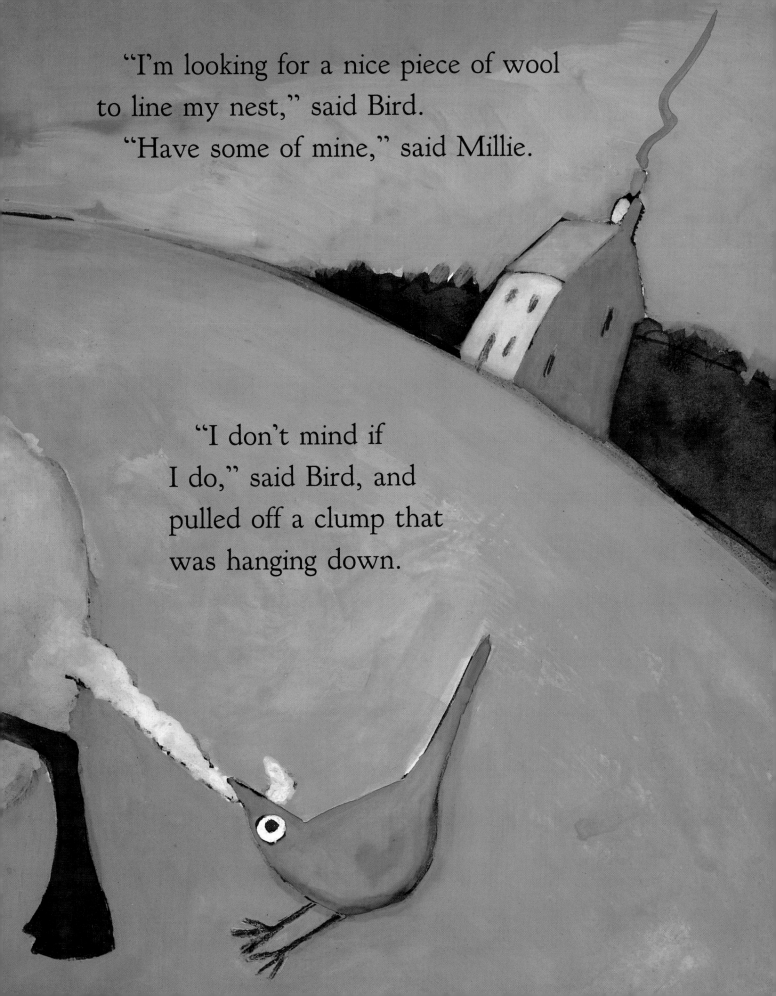

"I'm looking for a nice piece of wool
to line my nest," said Bird.
"Have some of mine," said Millie.

"I don't mind if
I do," said Bird, and
pulled off a clump that
was hanging down.

"I'm also looking for a nice clump for *my* nest," said Badger, who seemed to have appeared from nowhere.

"Help yourself," said Millie.

"And me," begged Rabbit.

"You, too," said Millie, and rubbed herself against a tree so that they could each get a nice clump of wool.

Soon all her wool was gone.

"Look at you," said Alma, who was
a sensible sheep. "Imagine giving away
your good coat. You look like a goat now."
But Millie was happy. She hopped and
skipped, skipped and hopped, higher than
before, because she felt as light as a
feather without her heavy woolly coat.

But that night it snowed. Large,
cold flakes landed on Millie's bare
back and made her shiver.
Bird wasn't cold.
Badger wasn't cold.
Rabbit wasn't cold, either.
But Millie was very, very cold.

"You can stay up here in the tree with me," said Bird. But Millie couldn't climb trees.

"You are welcome to stay with me," said Badger.

But Millie was too big to crawl into Badger's burrow.

She peered into Rabbit's
hole and sighed. It was too
crowded in there already.

"No problem," said a sly fox.
"Stay with me. I like goats."

"I'm not a goat," bleated Millie, and ran off.

When Mrs. Farmer
saw Millie, she sighed.
"I wanted that wool to knit
a nice cardigan," she said. "It's
lucky that I still have some
wool left over from last year."

That night Millie slept in Mrs. Farmer's warm kitchen. She dreamed that she was a goat.

Clickety-click went Mrs. Farmer's knitting needles, all night long.

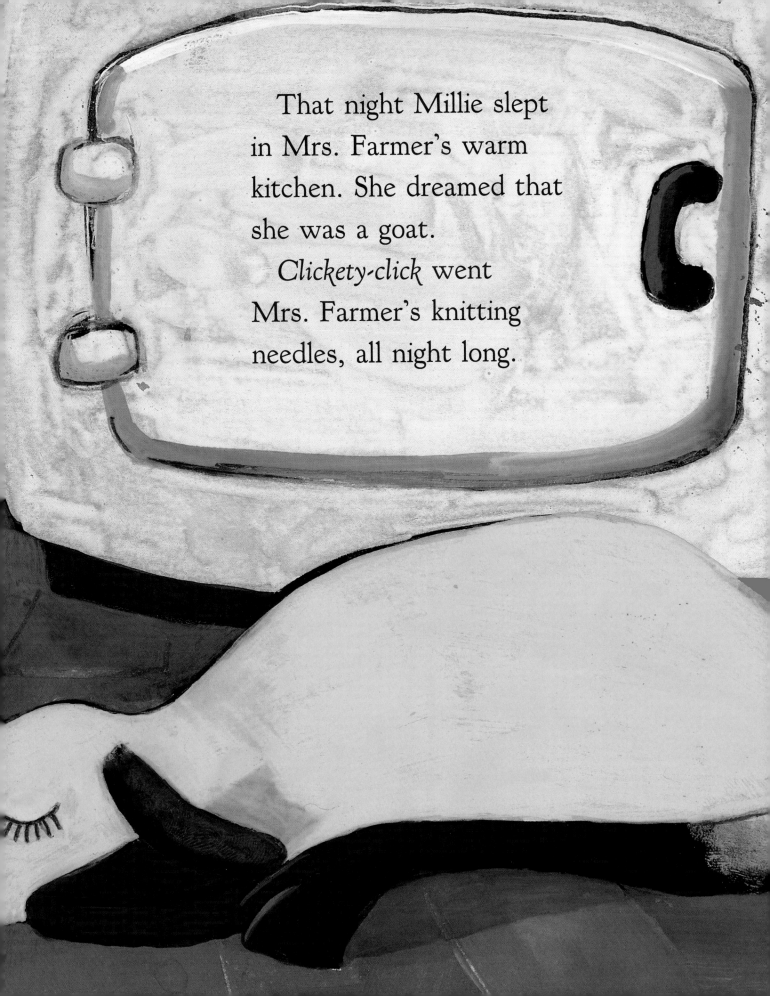

By morning, Mrs. Farmer had knitted a sweater for Millie. It was green, with yellow flowers and red hearts, and it fitted her perfectly.

Millie skipped back into
the field. She was warm again.

But there was a strand of wool hanging
down at the back of her new sweater.
And as she tried to pull it off, the
sweater unraveled itself a little.
"I could use a nice piece of
green wool," said Bird.

"Help yourself,"
said Millie.